Seal Skull

Written by Anne Curtis
Illustrated by Chris Corner

 Collins

I like to swim in the sea.
Mum says I'm like a seal in the water.

Today I found a skull washed up on the beach. It's smooth and white.

It seems to stare at me with dark, empty eyes.
It's a seal skull.

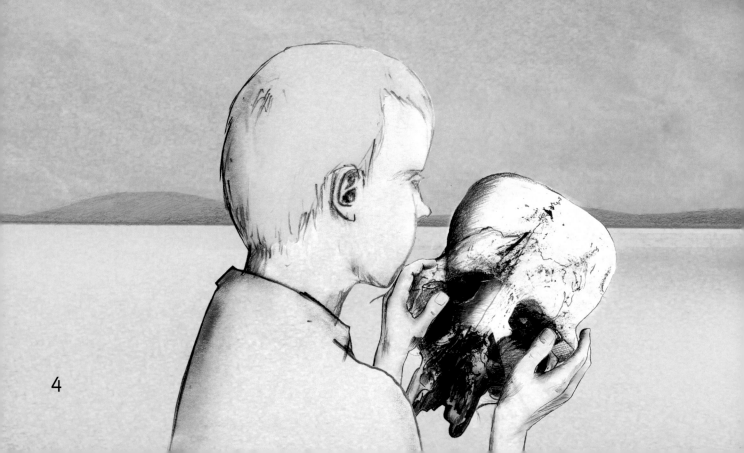

My room's full of dark shadows. Whenever Mum comes in, the dark shadows dive under my bed.

Mum says a storm is coming.
She thinks it's because of the skull.

Last night, I dreamt I was deep beneath
the waves. I saw the skull on the sea bed.
The dark shadows of seals were swimming
all around me.

When I wake, my clothes are wet.
There's salt on my skin and sand in my hair.

I can hear words like waves
crashing in my head
... a storm is coming
... a storm is coming.

10

must stop the storm.
'll take the skull back
o the sea.
'll make the shadows go.

The skull is in my hands.
As I walk towards the sea, the shadows
are following.

The seals are waiting.

13

The skull's power

Dark shadows dive under my bed.

Last night, I dreamt I was deep beneath the waves.

14

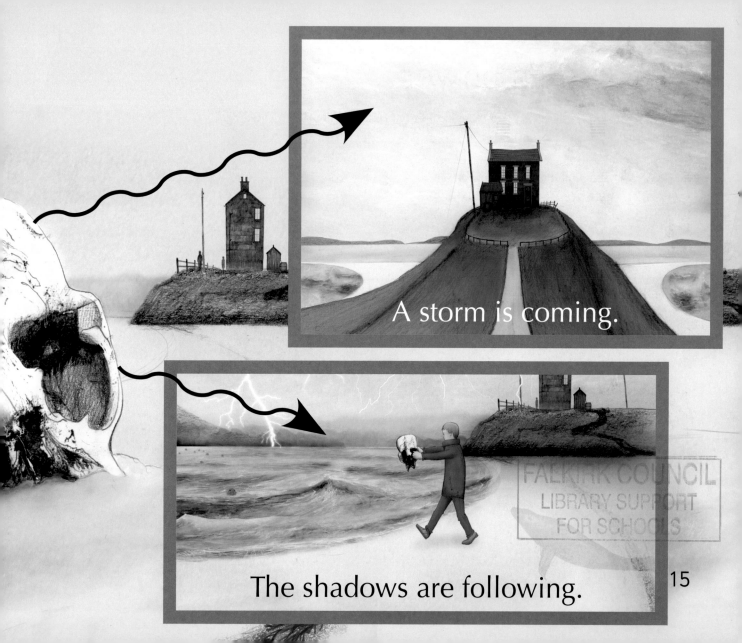

A storm is coming.

The shadows are following.

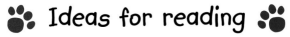 Ideas for reading

Written by Gillian Howell
Primary Literacy Consultant

Learning objectives: *(reading objectives correspond with Blue band; all other objectives correspond with Sapphire band)* use phonics to read unknown or difficult words; explore how writers use language for dramatic effects; compare the usefulness of techniques such as visualisation in exploring the meaning of texts; experiment with different narrative forms and styles to write their own stories

Curriculum links: Citizenship: Animals and us

High frequency words: water, white, with, bed, because, last, night, saw, were, when, there('s), must, take, back, make, as

Interest words: seal, skull, beach, empty, shadows, storm, clothes, following, waiting

Resources: paper, pens, papier maché

Word count: 177

Getting started

- Look at the cover and read the title and ask the children what sort of story they think this will be, for example, will it be funny, scary or exciting?

- Read the back cover blurb. Ask the children to say who the "I" of the story is. Ask the children to suggest whether the story will be in the past tense or present tense and why. If necessary, point out the words *today* and *It's* indicate the present tense.

Reading and responding

- Ask the children to read the story together. Remind them to use their phonic knowledge to work out new words.

- As they read, pause at significant events, e.g. on pp6–7, ask the children to say how they feel about the story. Ask them how the use of present tense verbs makes them feel, i.e. does it feel as if this is all happening *now*?

- Remind the children to look carefully at the pictures as they read to give them a better understanding of the story.

- Ask the children to read to the end of the book. Praise them for reading with expression and support children who need extra help.